Jill Dow trained at the Royal College of
Art. Since graduating she has worked as a
freelance illustrator specializing in natural
history, including the highly successful
series *Bellamy's Changing World*.
The *Windy Edge Farm* stories are the
first books she has both written
and illustrated.

Jill Dow lives in Thornhill, near Stirling,
Scotland, with her husband and their
two young children.

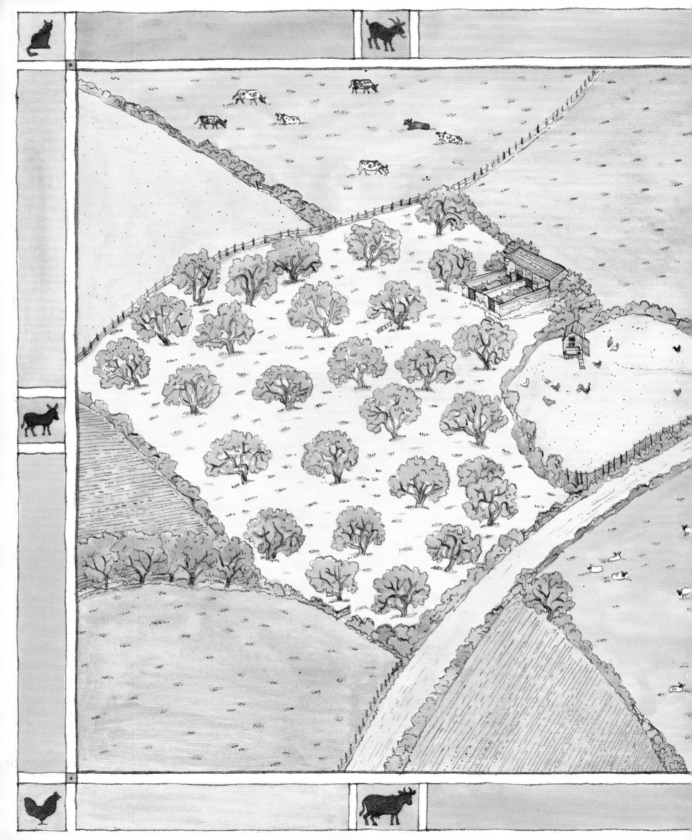

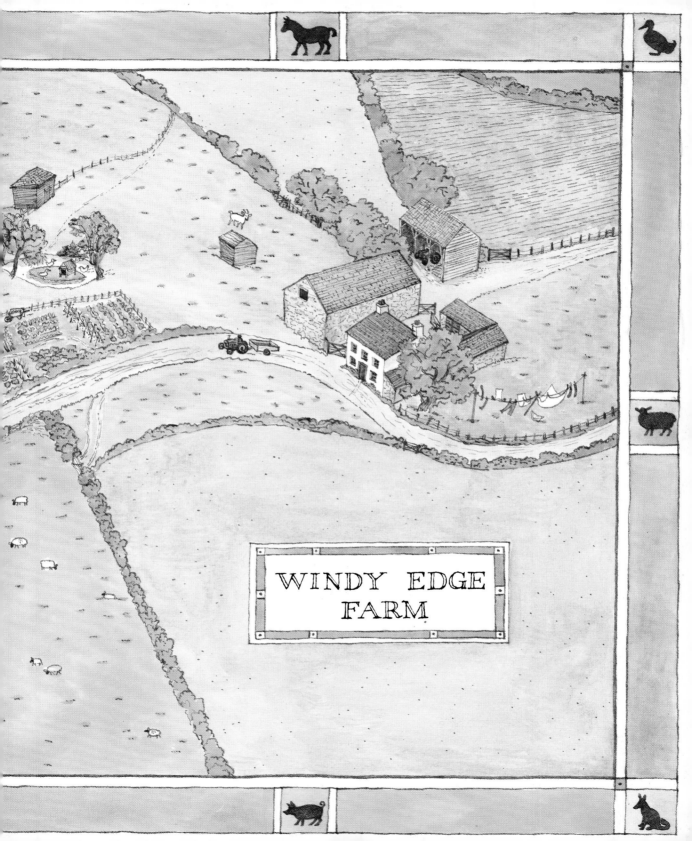

WINDY EDGE
FARM

For Callum

Text and illustrations copyright © Jill Dow 1992

First published in Great Britain in 1992 by
Frances Lincoln Limited, Apollo Works
5 Charlton Kings Road, London NW5 2SB

British Library Cataloguing in Publication Data
available on request

ISBN 0-7112-0729-1 hardback
ISBN 0-7112-0730-5 paperback

Set in Century Schoolbook by Goodfellow & Egan
Printed and bound in Hong Kong

3 5 7 9 8 6 4 2

WINDY EDGE FARM

PIGGY LITTLE'S HIDE & SEEK

Jill Dow

FRANCES LINCOLN

When Sarah, the sow at Windy Edge Farm, had seven piglets, Mr Finlay's son Angus gave them each a name.

The biggest was Guthrie. Then came Greta, Sophie, Sammy, Polly and Tommy. The last to be born, the smallest piglet of all, was Piggy Little. She was too weak to suckle from her mother so Mr Finlay took her into the kitchen and fed her from a bottle.

Angus made her a bed of straw in the washing basket, and she fell asleep in front of the stove.

Angus loved looking after Piggy Little. He fed
her every few hours, he changed the straw in
her basket and, if it was warm enough, he took
her outside to play in the sun.

With all his care, Piggy Little gained strength and grew quickly. In just a few days, she was almost as big as the other piglets, and Mr Finlay said she should go back to the pigsty. Sarah the sow seemed quite happy to welcome her back.

In the evening, Angus went to check that all was well. He found Piggy Little fast asleep, all snuggled up among her brothers and sisters. No need to worry about her keeping warm enough now!

After tea every day, Angus took a bucketful of scraps out to the sty.

He sat on the wall to watch the little pigs eat. He always knew Piggy Little by her floppy ear. Sometimes he scratched her back with a long stick. She loved that.

He was glad to see that Piggy Little had no trouble getting her fair share, even though she was the smallest.

One evening as he jumped down from the
pigsty, Angus kicked the door open by mistake.
Quick as a flash, the little pigs dashed out,
squeaking and squealing.

"Oh no!" Angus cried. "Come back! Come
back!" but by the time he had fastened the gate
to stop Sarah escaping, all the little pigs had
disappeared.

Angus ran through the orchard, hunting high and low.

There was Greta, gobbling fallen apples. Angus pounced!

But he didn't see Piggy Little . . .

All at once the hens were clucking and
squawking. Perhaps they were trying to tell
him something?

Angus raced over to the hen-house . . . and
caught Guthrie grunting happily as he raided
the grain bin!

But he didn't see Piggy Little . . .

Two little pigs back in the sty, but where could the others be? Suddenly Angus heard squeals of delight from the duck pond. Sophie and Sammy were wallowing in the mud!

Catching the two slippery piglets wasn't easy, and soon Angus was as filthy as they were. And he didn't see Piggy Little . . .

Someone was snorting and snuffling among the vegetables. Angus could see the goats nibbling the runner beans, but it didn't sound like them. He crept cautiously round the corner and saw . . . Polly, rooting up all the potatoes with her snout!

"Got you," shouted Angus in triumph. But he didn't see Piggy Little . . .

Two piglets still to find, and it was already getting dark . . . Angus watched the cows file out of the milking shed and racked his brains. Where could he look next?

CRASH! A milk churn toppled over, and there was . . . Tommy!

Angus snatched him up before Mr Finlay noticed what had happened. But he didn't see Piggy Little . . .

It was too dark to go on looking now. Angus
had found all the pigs – except the one he
loved most.

"Poor Piggy Little," he thought as he walked
sadly back towards the house. "Out in the cold
and dark, all alone."

He felt sadder still at the thought of all the explaining he had to do. Muddy face and clothes, spilt milk, stolen potatoes, and – worst of all – no Piggy Little.

It was a relief to find the kitchen empty. But
was there really no one there? A loud snuffly
snoring noise was coming from the washing
basket.

Angus ran to look – and there was Piggy
Little, fast asleep and very muddy, snuggled up
amongst the clean white sheets.

Angus smiled and tiptoed away. He didn't
care how angry anyone was with him now.
Piggy Little was found at last.

– The End –

OTHER **WINDY EDGE FARM** PAPERBACKS FROM FRANCES LINCOLN

"Lots of information woven into a very interesting text and the pictures
are most inviting." *Under Five* (The magazine of the Pre-school Playgroups Association)

BRIDGET'S SECRET
Every day Bridget the hen lays her brown speckled egg in a special place,
and Angus has to hunt high and low for it. But one day
Angus can't find Bridget's egg anywhere – nor can he find Bridget . . .
ISBN 0-7112-0570-1 £2.95

MOLLY'S SUPPER
Molly the cat stays out on the farm all day, and when evening comes
she's far away. Will Molly get home in time to be fed?
ISBN 0-7112-0569-8 £2.95

HEPZIBAH'S WOOLLY FLEECE
When the wind blows Hepzibah into a prickly bush, she has to wait
until she is rescued – and she wishes her woolly fleece were not so long . . .
ISBN 0-7112-0616-3 £2.95

WEBSTER'S WALK
Webster the farmyard duck takes all the other ducks on a walk to
the river. They are happy among the wild river birds, but when
a storm comes they miss their own pond at Windy Edge Farm.
ISBN 0-7112-0614-7 £2.95

**All these books are available at your local bookshop or newsagent, or by post from:
Frances Lincoln Paperbacks, P.O. Box 11, Falmouth, Cornwall.**

To order, send:
Title, author, ISBN number and price for each book ordered.
Your full name and address.
Cheque or postal order for the total amount, plus postage and packing.

UK: 80p for one book and 20p for each additional book ordered up to a £2.00 maximum.
BFPO: 80p for the first book, plus 20p for each additional book.
Overseas including Eire: £1.60 for the first book, plus £1.00 for the second book,
and 30p for each additional book ordered.

Prices and availability subject to change without notice.